After Engine Trouble

Good Morning Britain

Good Morning Britain!
It's grey and it's shit
it's Twitter for breakfast
it's hatred and hissy fits.

So reach for your phone
here's what you've missed
slap on the telly
scream at your kids.

Good Morning Britain!

Caffeine shot,
protein bomb,
the trans fat of news.
Here's Piers Morgan
and he's singing the blues:

You can't say anything these days
You can't say anything these days
And yet somehow you still manage to, Piers.

Good Morning Britain!
Where we don't like each other any more
we're trans activists in TERF wars
or brexit-boomers venting spleens
at all of Corbyn's triggered teens.
Incel Inside.
An empathy famine
from snowflakes to gammon:

No platform,
that's cancelled
she's cancelled,
err... he's cancelled
cranking up the public shame.
Cancellations *and* no platforms?
Shit, we're worse than Southern Trains!

Morrissey wakes and Morrissey says:
Whatever Anne-Marie has done,
I have done.
Gawd bless ya Stephen Patrick
everyone loves an expat Brexiteer.
Emigrants against the immigrants!
You couldn't make it up.

(well, obviously you could,
but why would you want to?)

Good Morning Britain
let's see those teeth
bent double under Grenfell's blackened jaw
Oh that thing was such an eyesore.
Now cuffs are slapped on wrists
that worked in hospitals for thirty years or more.
Yarlswood—that word again
Yarlswood—get back from whence you came.

Gooooooing home
They're going home
They're going...

Good morning Britain!
Where we're still voting like we always have
and all our contradictory data's
being mined and saved for later.
Someone call the Doctor.
From Cambridge Analytica to Jodie Whittaker
Good Morning Britain!

All this anger's making me angry
all this hatred is making me hate
all this anxiety is making me anxious
all this statementing has got me in a state.

So switch it off!
Put the mobile down, Luke.
Put the safety back on Ol' Betsy.
Step slowly away from the desk

I think I'll go to Lowestoft.
No, don't laugh
it's alright there—
paint flaking off the wooden fishing boats,
the statics watching from the Pakefield cliffs
it's mostly sky
with just a little bit reserved for us
a knee-deep sea and sand for miles and miles.
I'll go there and I'll swim today.
I'll sink beneath the shallow waves
and let the silence gently crush my chest
(that Temple Grandin knew her stuff).

And afterwards I'll find a caff
and listen in to little bits of chat
the foot-strut split and the yod-drop of this place.
I'll net their thoughts like butterflies
their heartbreaks, their bellyaches, and their wants
I bet I don't hear Brexit mentioned once.

I knew a man that let the news consume him:
he shouldered all that misery as if it were his own,
he shut out rooms,
disbarred himself from tables of his friends,
licked tin-foil sheets and stuck them on his windows.

Then, languishing in laptop light,
a breathless search for bullish blogs
to prove each cranky theory right
and sometimes he was right
and righteousness would flood the screen that night
but at what price?

Prayer

In concrete 1980's parks
my mother found a place to watch:
I need to keep an eye on you, she'd say.
And so she'd sit and swing her keys
or turn a Tube ad paperback
as I fell through an inky pool of time
to lose myself. Her eye on me: a length of twine
around my toe to pull me back for air.
I'll keep an eye on you. I'll keep an eye on you.

But I grew up, as we grow up
and scorned her eye and burned the twine,
dived drugged and drunk in dirty pools of bass.
I wasn't lost, I had myself
and lungs the size of concert halls.
I had it all, a stomach full of life
and all these eyes on me, an easy job, a wife.
I've finished, Miss, a smug glance at the clock.
I gazed down at my navel as if it were the world.

I had myself. I had myself.
So nothing much, as it turns out,
a twang of id, a shallow scrape of man.
It's just, some nights, when they're asleep,
I watch my sons and cannot breathe
to know they only have my eye on them.
What use my twine? What good this eye that darts around?
I take them to the park like nothing's wrong.
I watch them play and say: *I'll keep an eye on you.*

But when I sit and hold my knees
to watch them snoring silently
or see myself reflected in a screened call,
in debts that grow like Pigmyweed,
in callow words I barely mean
and sense there might be something ugly deep
down in my soul, I long to feel an eye on me,
a length of twine around my toe again.
So can you? Will you keep an eye on me
and should I need it, pull me up for air?

William Hague in a Baseball Cap

And she is going out tonight
and I am staying in
and I have never felt so wretched
breathless in her wake...

I imagine her two hundred miles away
behind the bullet-proof perspex
of her pre-club routine.
She is pink-lipped PVC
a bump of Taylor
a shot of Beyonce
blue ticks piling up and no time for reply.

While I am here,
carb-heavy, jim-jam-ready
haunting these rooms oh so fucking badly
no one is scared of me.
I am Baron Trump raiding the White House kitchen
for Pavlova after lights out.
I am meat paste sandwiches and funny uncles
cardigans and weather
ugly as a jailor, picking my nose.

While she is red carpet camera flashes:
stop, half-turn, smile.
Laugh with the Uber driver.
On the list / jump the queue.
She is calling BS on us all
she is Tank Girl, she is tear-gas honest,
she is a suffragette not looking back
at the explosion she has caused
for noble noble reasons.

While I, William Hague in a baseball cap
tap-tap at my Scrabble app
and check my bank balance,
still over-drawn. Bombay Bad Boy.
David Mitchell does a smug monologue on *Dave*.
The terror level has been raised to beige
as all the mirrors bevel outwards
and I catch myself stooping, stooping like my father.

And I can't even picture the bar she's in
but it's probably like 1920s Paris:
a razor-wire back-and-forth,
absinthe green, electrified.
And all the blokes are fucking Hemingway:
a dashing rugby squad of *enfant terribles*
the enfant terrible of Pre-op Post-feminism
the enfant terrible of Lexit Poetics
the enfant terrible of Pop-up Vietnamese Street Food
the enfant terrible of the Welsh Dark Net
flaunting the smoking ban, earnestly flippant.

While I,
I am the *enfant gluton* of this jar of pickled onions:
onesie, slanket, box-set, tissues.
I am the bottom half of the internet
I am a small town curry house the locals think is excellent
but is contemptible by city standards.
I am the shit Morrissey says in interviews
I am *Pale male and stale* and *Not all men*
I'm James Corden urging the British people to vote Remain
from the comfort of his LA TV studio
I am Dec

Yes, I'm Dec
I'm little Dec hosting the Take Away all on me tod

gold hearted and tin-eared,
a huge Valentines bear from Clinton Cards
HUG ME written across my gut
pedestalled in a window, half-price come March:
Hug me,
            Hug me,
                        Hug me.

Hotel Song

Unpack your box of cuspate truths
apply the morals of your folks.
Nietzsche cannot help you now
it's Church of England all the way.

Let these old crimes flood your lungs
from broken vows to blundered jokes
lie there on this rented bed
and tell yourself that this is you.

Forgotten faces. Misspelled names.
Your slipped-tongue twists of prejudice.
The tears you caused your eldest
when he found those photographs:

your morning suit, her light green dress
a silver frame, a date engraved
in winter jumpers by the Seine
or locked into a long embrace.

Excited boy: *It's Mum and you!*
That moment just before the tears.
No words for it, but up it comes
the truth he'd buried in his box.

You're that sallow silent pause
before the hug and best-fit words.
And yes, you're other things besides
but on this rented bed right now

you're that, you're only that.

The Ballad of the Dog

I'm in the boot. The cabbie's driving
through the pack of paps.
They slap the windows—*Is he in there?*
Is it true he's got the sack?

I'm in the boot. It's hot in here:
the booze sweats and the shame.
I paw the bare skin round my neck—
the collar's gone, gone too the chain.

I'm glad I'm in the boot. Outside
the sky is light-box grey.
It's endless, and I'm terrified
that when they pop this boot I'll float away.

*

Tethered to my mother first,
then God, then terraces:
learned loyalty at Highbury.
Then Cambridge honed my zealousness.

I toiled in the Treasury,
I gave my heartstrings hell—
slumped, sweaty at my desk through dinner,
in my cups until the bell.

My heart was lined with pay reviews
my scales were monetary—
I bathed my soul in Gunner goals
and dried it out in liturgy.

But then one May a landslide came
that left the Commons red.
Our new boss came to speak to us,
we lined up neat, I held my breath.

A spit-and-coal-dust union man
a stump-stomp when he spoke
with words that whistled, beckoning,
and something in my guts awoke.

For here was purpose, here was cause,
enough to slake my thirst
the blood-thrill of the terraces
dressed up in near-religious verse.

The poetry of campaign trails
it grabbed me by the nose
breathed hope into my hacking lungs
I longed to hear the governing prose.

And yet behind these noble words,
my master's heart was murk.
Want writhed in him, and now he'd found
a dog to do his dirty work.

Come Dog and do my bidding now
come Dog, forget your friends
if anyone stands in my way
you sink your bloody teeth in them.

But I shan't ask, so do not tell me.
This all ends with you.
Your sins will be absolved if we
achieve what we set out to do.

And so I came to flank my master
barking into phones
at editors and journalists
chasing tails and picking bones.

Then still and proud by stages giving
former friends the eye
Et tu! Et tu! I'll do for you
and I won't stop to question why.

For with that collar round my neck
all moral quandaries stopped.
Fine speeches scored my savagery.
I cleared a path right to the top.

Where still the blind-eye black-ops ran
as we both knew they would.
At night, my master told himself
his sins were for a greater good.

Just like I'd lie and tell myself
my sins were for that man.
And that man's conscience bore a weight
far heavier than mine could stand.

But everyone was out for us
our backs against the wall
choke-chain, rib kick, sick 'em, sick 'em,
muzzle-off and maul.

And each bite left me thirstier
each lie obscured more truth;
each frenzied mission riskier
until I left behind a tooth.

And O, the look my master threw me—
Set this mongrel free!
He washed his hands, his bloodless hands,
he washed his hands of me.

*

When the cabbie pops the boot
the weightlessness has gone.
I own the crimes that fill my gut,
my conscience dense as osmium.

Which weights my head as weeks drag by
and sags my savage jaw.
The phone which whistled constantly
is strangely silent in my paw.

My friends call round with news for me,
they rage and tell me how
I was betrayed, but all's not lost
for I am my own master now.

But dogs like me want weightlessness,
we long for someone's beck.
We beg the vast, black night for it—
I ache to feel that heavy chain around my guilty neck.

Pontardawe

The rushing rusty River Tawe
fattens out at Pontardawe
sends its earthy waters sluicing
foaming down the Swansea Valley

as I sit in the cutlery-rattle
tittle-tattle tabloid air of Sue's Cafe
and try to redirect that river
through my dusty heart.

I'm willing it to burst its banks
and sweep me off to somewhere new
to irrigate these seeds of thoughts
the summer has been full on, wretched hot and I am blocked.

There used to be a railway here
there used to be a steelworks too
right here, where I eat my eggs
and coal was mined up in those hills for years.

And yes, I know this song's been sung
this bit's been done to death
these derelict and disenfranchised towns
evoked by baity blokes up on the stump.

But I feel it all afresh when sitting here
or drifting down the Poundstretcher High Street.
Red Cross shops and on the sick—
we don't make anything anymore.

It all makes perfect sense on spreadsheets
where the labour's cheap, the lorries are laden.
They fire up the furnaces in Xinjiang
and ship it back across the seas to us.

So we don't make anything anymore.
Instead we take complaints or steam the milk
or put the customers on hold
and numb it with fluoxetine and box sets.

Because there is no substitute for making
and I'm aching for it here in Pontardawe.
Blowing oxygen through molten iron—
that white hot thrill of forging something new.

Gut

I never lost my gut and now I'm pushing 40.
These days, at the swimming pool, with the kids,
I look at the torsos of younger men and think:
even if I did all the weights,
and bought myself a head torch for night running,
bits of me would still sag.

My vanity put up a good fight
danced around like Prince Naseem Hamed.
But my ability to say *fuck it*
would always rouse itself
like Rocky in the twelfth,
Nigel Mansell at the British Grand Prix.

I suppose I should just give up.
Actually learn to love myself:
buy slacks and comfy jumpers,
frame a Rupi Kaur poem
and hang it in the downstairs loo.
But I won't.
Things just shouldn't be that easy.

Embrace the Wank

In defence of pretentiousness

Embrace the wank
Let the hipsters come.
Let them bring their complex coffee.
It's not their fault that you can't taste
the subtle hints of tangerine.
Of course you can't!
Your instant tastes like bong water.

Let them come on carbon fibre
penny farthings, scarfs a-flapping.
Allow their tweedy too-short trousers.
Praise their hempy eco-houses.
Millicent and Dick have built their dream home from used copies of the Guardian.
Hell yeah they have!

Embrace the wank
Yes, this film has subtitles
in fact they've all got subtitles
and non-linear narratives.
Deal with it.
They thought Milton was a heretic
You can't blame lattes for everything.

Look at them! The metropolitan elite!
mwah*mwah*mwah*mwah*
The Countryside Alliance might bristle
but I think they're as beautiful
as a non vocational degree.
Mais oui!

Fuck James May,
I want Alan Yentob,
Alan Yentob, Alan Yentob, Alan Yentob.

Maybe it's because you question nothing
you don't know what an answer looks like.

Embrace the wank
Break up common sense
into its component parts
and recycle it recklessly.
Bullshit to your back to basics
and your calling a spade a spade.
I haven't had enough of experts.
Where are my experts?
Bring me my experts!
Let me bathe in a pool of expert-jism.

Embrace the wank.
Manet's dad thought he was wasting his time as well.
Why can't you be normal like Nigel Farage?
The greatest trick the devil ever pulled
was convincing the world he liked a pint.
So pass me that cocktail menu: *I'll have a 'Brutalism'*
gin from the earthenware bottle.

Embrace the wank
Yes, I do call this a haircut
so what if I have empathy for my chair?
My partner,
yes my *partner,*
my *partner*
learned Russian so she could read Mayakovsky in the original
you bought an Ed Sheeran DVD.
It's not about being better,

just don't look at us
like somehow *we're* the ludicrous ones.

Embrace the Wank
Gwyneth Paltrow—I salute thee
I'd rather smoke crack
than eat cheese from a tin.
These are my sons:
Hopscotch and Entwhistle
This is daughter:
Keith.
Don't they look sweet
suspended in formaldehyde?

Lady Gaga—keep it up!
Who does she think she is?
Fucking GOD! That's who!
What of it?

Let them eat millet
with carpaccio of stoat
smear it across a brick
and take out a mortgage on it.
Come on Sting grab your lute
and let's all do the wounded peacock.

Embrace the wank
Yes that poem bored me too
but at least it was something new
so play it again.
This wank is how we change.
Otherwise we'd still be wearing ruffs.
And yes, I know that fella over there
with the handlebar moustache
and the bicycle clips

IS wearing a ruff
but fuck it,
you're not in Slough now, darling.

Keep your patriarchal statues
Keep Adrian's predictable stag
Keep your decent hard-working, normal, hard-working, decent,
hard-working normal families
Keep your Sunday night drama in which Nicola Walker looks
tired.
I'm happy in my floatation tank
Do you have any non-dairy milk?
Sure no one *needs* a pushchair that complex
but fuck me, it's glorious
like a goth on a beach.

Embrace the wank
Fine take your wellies
I'm wearing my Louis XIV slippers.
It's only Glastonbury
I'm sure there's paths.

Don't look like that,
cut off the extra sleeve
and they'll sell it in Primark next year.
You'll buy one.

Look, for every Shia LaBoeuf
there's a David Lynch.
By all means, you call it a day
but, for fuck's sake,
let the rest of us play.

Troll

Some nights, I imagine my foes throw a party,
they hire a sports bar and take it in turns
to read my worst poems in mock plummy tones.

My best mate from sixth-form does an excellent me
Uncanny! cry ex-colleagues jack-knifed in giggles
at all my most cloying political rants.

And Luke Wright, The Cricketer, is there with his Ted Talk.
Sometimes they tweet me in error, he LOLs
This poetry thing? I mean, is it a thing?

And there's my ex-wife holding court in the corner.
Old girlfriends guffaw at her elbow. One wheezes:
I think he just thinks that ...well ... that's how you do it.

My internet trolls live-tweet the event.
The hashtag #ThoseTrousers trends for 6 minutes.
The singer from Right Said Fred Skypes in from Scunthorpe.

My sons raise a chorus of *Daddy's a Poo-poo*
(It's under rehearsed and it goes down quite poorly)
That Guardian critic just closes her Moleskine.

And even my mother puts in an appearance,
blowing her latte tight-lipped and aloof.
This isn't my fault, she thinks. *This isn't my fault.*

My dad arrives later as things are subsiding
he makes a brief turn of the room, and then leaves.
He gets it, it's just that he doesn't like parties.

O! but that sports bar is fetid with glee!
The agent who promised he'd get me on *Buzzcocks*
toasts the producer who didn't book me!

And look! The anonymous internet user
who once said I "badly needed sterilising."
He looks at my sons with a shake of his head.

A glorious gaggle. United in hatred.
And there I am, lurking behind the false mirror,
observing their pleasure, my kecks round my knees.

After Engine Trouble

We had stopped for crisps
so at least we didn't look like twats
under foil blankets on the hard shoulder
eliciting pity as steam rose.

And although it wasn't my fault
I kept apologising for the car
I knew you were tired
and Olive had school in the morning.

But you reached beneath the passenger seat
and produced a wardrobe full of silver linings:
we had that blanket from the National Trust shop
and an endless supply of Pringles.

Even after all these months
I have to remind myself that this is something new
that you won't roll your eyes at me
and sigh, as if you threw your life away.

The AA man arrived like someone's Dad
blew into his hands and talked in bloke
two hundred quid later we coughed
onto the carriageway, better off.

The Lay-bys and Bypasses

I claim to know this country
stretch my vowels across its contours
and detonate my consonants on its illicit missteps.
King among the little Brits!
I know this place of pubs, I say
I know this place
let me recite for you

and tell you how we're cast adrift from Europe
mad upon the seas we claim to rule.
Sat around the port, we shiver:
red coats threadbare at the elbows
pith helmets a-brim with butts and sick.

The sun is up again
and we've just three strings on our violin
split ends springing from the bow
we're coming down
drifting down the corridors
clutching faded photo books
but listen now, our song's still beautiful.

Pray silence for our drunk thumbs—
this is Britain.
And I'm in sync with all of it
I can tell it like it is.

Last week I drove from Sheffield to Deal
five hours without a stop
save pissing in a lay-by outside Luton
my mind a-swim in caffeine pop
I didn't use a map.
Oh no! I know this place, I thought,
I know this place.
But what do I know?
I know the motorways,
I know the lay-bys and the bypasses
I lay-by
I by pass

There's life behind those conifers
that I will not observe.

I spit my wit then split.
I pinch myself to stay awake.
Two empty car seats in the back
some days I just see skeletons.
In a motor
they can't hear you when you scream.

I live the life a wide-eyed child chose for me.
Perhaps you do as well?
Rickety old sleeper trains
we trundle on
we miss the points.

So here I am:
a different strip of tarmac each night
a hundred miles from home
watching seagulls swoop like stunt kites
on a coast that's not my own.

I try my best to make some sense of that
I tally up the good days with the bad
I keep my fires smouldering
I shovel on the poems and the admin,
the triumphs of my children.

I roll my terrors round my palm like Baoding balls:
the way the house feels after 9pm
the Christmas morning lie-in
the gigabytes of smiles I dare not open.

Because I know what happy is:
a carload full of friends on a festival weekend
a phone call every night
drifting off, our fingertips in touch
tearing through the long grass with my boys
or standing waist deep in September sea
gasping with the cold
loose lacerated lungs
and a belly full of love.

That time I tumbled from a train in Taunton
hungover and hilarious
it must have been June
it really must, the sky was huge and blue.
I just adored it
so as it swallowed me,
I swallowed it right back
and down the hatch went all of England with it.
It knocked me to my knees
thinking: *Yes*
I'm here, I'm here
I never thought I would be
but I'm here.

O I claim to know this country
but all I do is make it in my image:
squeeze it into spray-on jeans,
file its teeth, distill its spleen,
take potshots at its pompousness for sport.

I love and loathe it,
like I love and loathe myself
and yes, I know it,
because I know myself.
I know myself.